P9-ASB-589

Mother Goose's

FACSIMILE EDITION OF THE MUNROE AND
FRANCIS "COPYRIGHT 1833" VERSION

Melodies

With an Introduction and Bibliographic Note by

E. F. Bleiler

DOVER PUBLICATIONS, INC., NEW YORK

Published in Canada by General Publishing Company, Ltd.,
30 Lesmill Road, Don Mills, Toronto, Ontario.
Published in the United Kingdom by Constable and Company, Ltd.,
10 Orange Street, London WC 2.

This Dover edition, first published in 1970, is an un-
abridged and unaltered republication of the work published by Munroe & Francis in Boston, and entered in the
year 1833 in the Clerk's Office of the District Court of
Massachusetts. For this Dover edition E. F. Bleiler has
written a new Introduction and Bibliographic Note,
both of which give additional information concerning
the Munroe & Francis editions.

International Standard Book Numbers:
(Clothbound) 0-486-22659-X
(Paperbound) 0-486-22577-1
Library of Congress Catalog Card Number: 77-108034

Manufactured in the United States of America
Dover Publications, Inc.
180 Varick Street
New York, N.Y. 10014

INTRODUCTION TO THE
DOVER EDITION

THE BOOKS

Mother Goose is truly the Mother of Mystery in books. Despite decades of study by folklorists and literary historians, almost any significant question that can be asked about either the Mother Goose books or individual rhymes must be answered in the same way: not known.

What does the term Mother Goose mean, and how did it originate? The best that can be said is that it is not English in origin but French, and that *conte de la mère l'oye* around the middle of the seventeenth century meant a tall tale or a nursery fairy tale. Nothing is really known about the origin or significance of the term, although students of French folklore have tried to identify *Mère l'oye* with various figures in French history and tradition. None of this has been very convincing.

In 1697 Charles Perrault's *Histoires ou contes du tems passé, avec des moralitéz* was published. The frontispiece of this book, which is one of the world's classic fairy tale collections, showed a woman spinning, presumably telling tales to a small group of children, with the legend *contes de ma mère loye*. This is the first known association of the term Mother Goose with printed children's literature, but it should be noted that Perrault's works are literary fairy tales in prose and rhyme and not nursery rhymes. For English translations of the fairy tales, which began to appear in 1729, the title was variously rendered as *Tales of Passed Times by Mother Goose* or *Mother Goose's Tales*. This would seem to be the first use of the term Mother Goose in English.

When was the first Mother Goose collection of nursery rhymes printed? Again, this is not known. The earliest surviving collection, not under the title Mother Goose, is avowedly a second volume: *Tommy Thumb's Pretty Song Book, Voll. 2*, which contained among other rhymes "Little Tommy Tucker," "There Was an Old Woman liv'd under a Hill," and a curious variant of "Sing a Song of Sixpence":

> Sing a Song of Sixpence,
>   A Bag full of Rye,
> Four and twenty
>   Naughty boys,
> Bak'd in a Pye.

This tiny book, known only in a single cropped copy in the British Museum, is not dated, although it is usually placed around 1745. Volume One has not survived.

When did the first nursery rhyme book entitled Mother Goose appear? Once more, not known, but a wealth of research has led to fairly sound speculation. Some time in the late middle eighteenth century, the British publisher John Newbery, now remembered as the pioneer in children's literature, printed a small collection of nursery rhymes entitled *Mother Goose's Melody*. The year 1765 is accepted as a reasonable hovering date for this book. Unfortunately, no copies of this first edition (or records of its publication) survive. If it was identical with the second edition of 1791, it would have been a book of 96 pages, with the first ten pages devoted to a tongue-in-cheek prefatory matter, adult in tone, and the last twenty to songs from Shakespeare. The pages between would have contained fifty-one nursery rhymes, each followed by a mock-serious maxim:

High, diddle, diddle,
  The Cat and the Fiddle,
The Cow jump'd over the Moon;
  The little Dog laugh'd
To see such Craft,
  And the Dish ran away with the Spoon.

It must be a little Dog that laugh'd, for a great
Dog would be ashamed to laugh at such Nonsense.

Oliver Goldsmith, it is a fair supposition, was responsible for this 1765 Mother Goose. He was associated with Newbery at this time, and had also written his *Goody Two-Shoes* for Newbery. Various small points known about Goldsmith, such as rhymes that he liked to quote and children's games that he liked to play, add up to reasonable conviction that Goldsmith was the first Mother Goose to be known by that name.

When did Mother Goose first appear in America?

Again, not known. Its second appearance, however, was in 1794, when Isaiah Thomas of Worcester, Massachusetts, printed Newbery's book for the second time, almost verbatim. The only significant change that Thomas made was a change of location from London to Boston:

> Se saw, sacaradown,
> Which is the way to *Boston* Town?
> One Foot up the other Foot down,
> That is the way to *Boston* Town.

Judging from early advertisements, Thomas must have printed his first edition some time around 1785. An incomplete copy of this first American edition survives.

Mother Goose was next reborn, in her most important incarnation of all, in Boston, Massachusetts, in the 1820's and 1830's. There Edmund Munroe and David S. Francis, booksellers and publishers, who were later famous for their stereotype piracies of British books, established the first important Mother Goose books in America. As usual, it is not possible to give publishing details about their early Mother Goose books beyond what can be reconstructed. Boston publishing at this time was parochial rather than national, and in any case no one was interested in keeping records of children's books.

Munroe and Francis published the first modern Mother Goose at some time around 1825. Entitled *Mother Goose's Quarto, or Melodies Complete* (although it was not really a quarto, but a very small book), it was the largest collection of children's rhymes to have appeared to date, some 128 pages. It contained most of the verses that are well remembered, and it omitted for the most part the coy Goldsmithian peculiarities that disfigured the Newbery and Thomas publications. It was frankly a book for children, not for patronizing adults.

Mother Goose's Quarto, which survives in a single known copy, introduced many new rhymes to the American Mother Goose assembly: "Little Boy Blue," "Bye, Baby Bunting," "Rain, Rain, Go Away," "The Lion and the Unicorn," "Lady-Bird, Lady-Bird," "Little Miss Muffett," "Peter Piper," "Diddle, Diddle Dumpling, My Son John," "Taffy Was a Welshman," and "Peter, Peter, Pumpkin Eater." Many of these, of course, had appeared in other books not officially Mother Goose.

Occasionally strange variants appear in *Mother Goose's Quarto:*

> Ride a cock horse to Banbury Cross,
>   To see an old woman jump on a black horse

> See, saw, sacradown, sacradown,
>   Which is the way to Boston town?
> One foot up the other foot down
>   That is the way to Boston town.
> Boston town's chang'd into a city,
>   But I've no time to change my ditty.

Boston became a city in 1822.

This Munroe and Francis *Mother Goose's Quarto,* however, was not an important book in itself. As far as can be determined, it was not reprinted, and it left no perceptible trace in the popular memory. The book that later generations remembered as the Mother Goose of their childhood was *Mother Goose's Melodies*, copyright and published in January, 1833.*

This second Munroe and Francis Mother Goose was based largely on *Mother Goose's Quarto*. It was condensed to 96 pages, rearranged internally, and in part reillustrated. It went through several editions and many printings, and it remained in print up until at least the 1860's.

It is pointless to dispute which is the first Mother Goose book, since the trail of children's books is so complex and the corpus of nursery verses accreted so gradually over almost a century of publishing in England and America. But if one must select a single Mother Goose book as the "original," this Munroe and Francis 1833 volume is the strongest candidate. It is a rich, modern collection, well conceived and well produced. It was almost national in its distribution (as opposed to the local distributions of the various reprintings of Newbery's volume), and it set off a chain of imitations, piracies, and similar collections that continues to the present. It was largely responsible for the adoption of Mother Goose in America as the supreme children's poet, as opposed to her early British rivals, Gammer Gurton, Tom Thumb, Nurse Lovechild, or others. It is also a book of classical stature that can be read today for its own sake, differing in this respect greatly from the earlier collections, which are mostly curiosities. Although it is a point on a continuum, it is the most important point.

We may conjecture fairly safely on the way that the

* See Bibliographic Note beginning on page 99 of this volume.

Munroe and Francis establishment prepared *Mother Goose's Quarto* and *Mother Goose's Melodies*, even though no documentation has survived. Their editorial approach was bibliographic rather than folkloristic. The editors made use of earlier books, often showing considerable resourcefulness and some exercise of judgment, rather than collecting fresh material from children or from their own memory—although there is always a possibility that an occasional verse came from oral tradition. "I love little pussy" seems to have been first collected in one of the later editions of the *Mother Goose's Melodies*, in a somewhat different version from that of the *Juvenile Miscellany* of 1830. From the Newbery-Thomas publications Munroe and Francis picked up a core of material, almost all of the original contents, although they dropped a few in later editions of *Mother Goose's Melodies*. The other most important source was a British collection, *Song for the Nursery* (1818 edition, printed by William Darton). Individual poems came from many other sources. It is a curious note that despite the jibe at Mrs. Follen in the first edition of *Mother Goose's Melodies*, Munroe and Francis reprinted her verses "Cock, cock, cock, cock, I've laid an egg" and "Three Little Kittens" in later editions. Many other sources seem to have been used.

This process of selection does not mean that the Munroe and Francis editorial policy was perfunctory piracy. The editors often modernized language, removed dialect where it was an unnecessary impediment, and changed texts slightly, from edition to edition, if they felt a new version was better. For example, the first edition of *Mother Goose's Melodies* uses basically the same text for "There was an old woman tost up in a blanket" as does Isaiah Thomas:

> There was an old woman tost up in a blanket,
>   Seventeen times as high as the moon,
> What she did there no mortal can tell,
>   But under her arm she carried a broom . . .

This was probably also the text that Goldsmith used to sing to his friends. The later editions, however, have

> There was an old woman tost up in a blanket,
>   Seventy times as high as the moon,
> What she did there I cannot tell you,
>   But in her hand she carried a broom. . . .

The new text probably came from *Songs for the Nursery*.

In illustration, too, Munroe and Francis took pains with their Mother Goose books. They retained the studio of Abel Bowen, the introducer of wood engraving to the Boston area, to illustrate many of the verses. Bowen himself did several of the cuts, and his associates did others. A former apprentice of Bowen's, Nathaniel Dearborn, created the image of Mother Goose for the cover and dedication page reprinted here. As new editions emerged, the focus of work seems to have shifted in part to the New York area, probably because of the New York distributor, C. S. Francis. Thus, whereas *Mother Goose's Quarto* was mostly the work of Bowen and associates, the first edition of *Mother Goose's Melodies* contained several engravings by Dr. Alexander Anderson of New York, who has as good claim as anyone to have been the first man to practice white-line wood engraving in the United States. In later editions Anderson contributed more illustrations, the most appropriate series on pages 14, 15, 21, 22, 31, 41, 45, and 76 signed with his initials, AA. If these engravings are examined under a lens, they reveal not only remarkable craftsmanship but a pawkish, sardonic vein of humor equal to that of the best British satirical engravers of the period. In the last known printing of *Mother Goose's Melodies* by Munroe and Francis, circa 1845, the New York collector and engraver Samuel Avery appears twice.

The illustrators of Mother Goose, in general, tried to establish a working compromise between originality and familiarity. In the earliest American Mother Goose, that of Isaiah Thomas, the illustrations were slavishly copied from British prototypes. In the Munroe and Francis books, however, there was more room for new work. When Anderson (?) recut the illustration for "Rub-a-dub-dub, Three men in a tub," he retained the idea of the old English illustration, but reinterpreted it. Other illustrations are wholly new, obviously cut to fit the verse. This, of course, is somewhat unusual, for all too often a publisher of a children's book simply took whatever stock cuts were available and jammed them into (often inappropriate) association with the text. On the other hand, Abel Bowen reengraved the ghoulishly grotesque "Man in the Moon" cut from Darton's *Songs for the Nursery*, without much change.

Because of the exigencies of woodblock printing, the illustrations were not always stable from one book to another or one edition to another. Blocks could become worn or damaged, and became warped at the edges if not properly dried. Or perhaps the art director of the time thought they looked better trimmed. In any case, between the first version of *Mother Goose's Melodies* (1833) and the copy owned by Dover Publications and reprinted here, many originally square cuts were routed down to irregular shapes, and borders were shaved off. In most cases this does not affect the meaning of the illustration, but there are three curious results. The cut on page 11 was originally a full rectangle, with another range of dishes on the shelf, and two candlesticks on the mantle. If the cut in the Dover edition is examined closely, the remains of the second candlestick can be seen on the left. On page 38 the cat originally was sitting in a window frame, not floating in the air. On page 58, the riders were making their way at night through a heavy rain; this rainy background was completely routed out.

Between editions and printings, it may be assumed, the woodblocks were stored in a box somewhere, and individual blocks could "wander." In such cases a new illustration roughly suitable to the verse might be put into the page at the last minute. "Bobby Shaftoe" shows such a sequence of illustration. It was originally illustrated by a signed engraving (not simply initialed, according to Whitmore) in *Mother Goose's Quarto*. Possibly this was lost. The earlier printings of *Mother Goose's Melodies* show the fine maritime scene on page 55, which is not particularly appropriate, though interesting. This was eventually omitted in later printings. Similarly, the glowering rabbit (Bowen?) on page 84 was eventually changed to a tricky split illustration. Presumably the children did not care.

Most of the Munroe and Francis cuts fit the verses, and were presumably drawn to specification. The exceptions are occasionally more interesting than the concordances. The series of Empire-style cuts on pages 16, 47, 52, 62, 67, 69 and 81, which were new to *Mother Goose's Melodies* and were added gradually through new printings, obviously do not fit the verses. The illustration on page 81 does not show "Three brethren out of Spain," but two assassins and perhaps their victim, perhaps their employer. Pages 62, 67, and 69 show Italian scenes from a late Gothic romance. Presumably Munroe and Francis owned this series from another publication, possibly a broadside, and put them to service.

An exceptionally charming note is the illustration on page 38, which shows a child holding a small children's book. This is the living situation of Mother Goose.

The third Munroe and Francis Mother Goose book, *Chimes, Rhymes, and Jingles; or, Mother Goose's Songs, Being the Remainder of her Melodies*, was entered for copyright in 1845; one of the two surviving copies has a dated inscription from February, 1846. While other publishers used the title later, we have no knowledge of the printing history of the Munroe and Francis edition.

In style *Chimes, Rhymes, and Jingles* is a Victorian book through and through, very different from the early nineteenth-century style of the other Mother Goose books. Designed by Hammatt Billings, possibly as his first major work, with blocks by A. Hartwell, it was obviously creatively influenced in design by contemporary British book publishing. In content, however, it is less original. While the subtitle claims that the book is a new collection of verses, this is not really true. Some pieces are taken from the earlier *Mother Goose's Melodies*, and most of the other material is lifted bodily from J. O. Halliwell's *Nursery Rhymes of England*, the third edition of which Munroe and Francis had printed in stereotype (pirated from England) in 1843. Some of the material taken from Halliwell is unusual. Instead of "Little Miss Muffett who sat on a tuffet," *Chimes, Rhymes, and Jingles* has "Little Mary Ester, sat upon a tester"; in "Ding, Dong, Bell" Little Tommy Lin threw pussy into the well, while "Dog with long snout" pulled her out. "Sing a Song of Sixpence" has a final couplet:

> Jenny was so angry she knew not what to do—
> She put her finger in her ear and crack'd it
>   right in two.

With this overdesigned assortment of secondary rhymes, ballad fragments, and miscellaneous verse, the Munroe and Francis series of Mother Goose books comes to an end.

THE VERSES

The Mother Goose rhymes themselves are the literary cut-me-downs and hand-me-downs of the centuries. Outside of being associated with children, they have little in common with one another. Sometimes international among European children in form and subject matter, they show a veritable hodgepodge of origins: decayed songs and rhymes of adult origin, often literary; riddles; rhythmoids for games; indicants for processes; sound-effect verse and much else.

As with other traditional literature, most of the time no author is known for them, no place of origin, and often no circumstances of ultimate meaning. The important Mother Goose rhymes that can be traced to an author and origin-point can almost be numbered on one's digits. "Mary Had a Little Lamb," for example, was written by Mrs. Sara Hale of Boston, who first published it in 1830, even though it has since joined the faceless company; and "Twinkle, Twinkle, Little Star" is known to be by Jane Taylor [1806]. But such poems are very much the exception.

Certain scholars and enthusiasts have assumed that the rhymes once had meaning in a historical sense, and have devoted ingenuity to finding hidden memories and meanings. To mention one of the most famous of these attributions: "Mary, Mary, Quite Contrary" has often been aligned with Mary, Queen of Scots. "Silver bells and cockle shells" is taken to refer to her Roman Catholic ceremonial and her fancy dress, and the "pretty maids all in a row" to her four well-known maids-in-waiting. A counterline, often quoted, "With cuckolds all in a row," has been taken to refer to the moral degeneracy of her court. Unfortunately, there is no reason to accept this fine interpretation.

A similar story is told of Jack Horner, who sat in a

corner. He has been identified with a member of the Horner family, favorites of Henry VIII, who swindled themselves into valuable property at the dissolution of the monastic holdings. According to fancy, which is probably based on the nursery rhyme, rather than vice versa, Horner was conveying deeds to the court. He surreptitiously withheld one for himself, which in the confused succession he managed to retain. It is even narrated that Horner was conveying the deeds in a pie crust and wriggled a parchment out through a crust-hole!

Yet even though these examples are suspect, we can occasionally see modern history structuring itself into the classical rhyme forms. "Bobby Shaftoe's gone to sea" seems to have been a political campaign song for a Parliamentary candidate in 1761. In our own day two major rhymes have joined the corpus, both authorless, both typical in form: "Charlie Chaplin went to France, To teach the ladies how to dance," and even more familiar:

> Lizzie Borden took an axe,
>> And gave her mother forty whacks;
> When she saw what she had done,
>> She gave her father forty-one.

Other sources are really more important than history as ultimates for the rhymes. Many rhymes are altered, fragmented, decontexted descendants of adult material: broadside ballads, stage songs, folksongs, and similar material. "'I'm going a milking, sir,' she said" was known as a slightly bawdy broadside in the early seventeenth century. And "Tweedledee and Tweedledum," according to the usual interpretation, originated in an eighteenth-century pasquin concerning Handel in London. Many nursery rhymes are in a way functional, providing rhythm or structural breaks in play situations or dances. "Ring-a-ring of roses" (Ring around the rosie) is an obvious example, where the ring dance is followed by a tumble on "achew, achew (ashes, ashes) we all fall down." "London Bridge" is another such dance or game song modified into a nursery rhyme. Here again we see the curious history of nursery songs and games: very much the same game, with comparable verses, has been identified in every major Western European culture from the Middle Ages to the present. Some scholars have tried to find the one single bridge that did break, historically. Others have interpreted the game as a survival in folk culture of the memory of human sacrifice connected with bridge building. A more reasonable explanation is that it was simply a game, diffused in the late Middle Ages, in which dancing couples formed bridges, with no external meaning or associations.

Another functional nursery rhyme is to be found in the many counting rhymes in Mother Goose. These are simple exercises in recreational mathematics to select an individual impartially, since, practically speaking, one cannot easily locate "it" before the rhyme is ended. Of these "Eeny, meeny, miney, mo" is the best-known, while "Hickory, dickory, dock" was formerly another. In both these rhymes the seeming nonsense words conceal memories of old pre-English counting systems of Celtic origin. "Hickory, dickory, dock," for example, is a garbled version of the numerals eight, nine, and ten.

Many Mother Goose rhymes were lullabies; others were riddles, similar in matter and form to adult riddles; others, like "Lady-Bird, Lady-Bird" might be classified as juvenile magic. Instructional rhymes are also found, such as "A was an Archer" and "One two, buckle my shoe." Certain verses were distractional, serving to keep children quiet, and were often accompanied by things to be done. "This little piggy went to market" is often recited while grasping the toes or fingers of the child. "Pattacake, Pattacake" is usually recited with hand-clapping, while Goldsmith himself played "Two Little Dicky Birds" with a complicated finger play involving paper. Other rhymes such as "Goosey-goosey, Gander," "Hi diddle, diddle, the Cat and the Fiddle," and "Higglety, Pigglety, Pop, the dog has eaten the mop" (S. Goodrich, 1846) represent pure fancy, although some folklorists are loath to accept a verse that has no meaning.

By now it should be obvious that many Mother Goose rhymes are not modern in origin. The Opies, whose work on nursery rhymes really subsumes almost everything we know, tabulated the verses according to historical evidence, and concluded that a quarter of the verses originated before 1600, another quarter in the seventeenth century, and another forty per cent in the eighteenth century. Occasional references to Mother Goose rhymes are found in the early major authors, a couple in Shakespeare, including possibly "Ding, Dong, Bell," and "Sing a Song of Sixpence" in Beaumont and Fletcher.

THE NEW MOTHER GOOSE

"When the rhymes were published, the kids began to sing—" is not quite true. Publication of the Mother Goose verses, particularly in America, has set in operation a series of new (or strengthened) processes that have changed the essence of the rhymes themselves. For generations the publishers have striven mightily to keep the Mother Goose rhymes as songs, since a fair number were once associated with tunes. Newbery included one brief section of music, while the later nineteenth-century editions, from Walter Crane on, have become more and more ambitious in including traditional or new tunes and accompaniments. But the reading public has had none of this, and the musical element has tended to disappear, except as folklorists and folk-doers have fostered it.

The action or secondary aspects of the verses also have tended to recede as the book rather than the nurse or playmate has become the source for the nursery rhyme. Few of us remember "Pease porridge hot, pease porridge cold" as a clapping game, as studies call it, or "See-saw, Margery Daw" as a rhythm verse to a seesaw board. Many of the group games have been divorced from their verses. We still remember "London Bridge is falling down" and "Here we go round the mulberry bush" as games, though faintly, but many other rhymes that once accompanied games and dances have become skeletonized to recitation verses. "Oranges and Lemons" ("The Bells of London'') is a typical example:

> Oranges and lemons,
>> Say the Bells of St. Clement's.
> You owe me five farthings,
>> Say the bells of St. Martin's.
> When will you pay me?
>> Say the bells of Old Bailey.*

This culminates in

> Here comes a candle to light you to bed,
> Here comes a chopper to chop off your head.

This verse accompanies a complex series of movements, which conclude in a mock decapitation. The action of this game is well recorded, with many variants; Mrs. Gomme, in her *Traditional Games of England, Scotland and Ireland*, devotes ten pages to it. Yet in America it would seem that the game situation is not well known, and the rhyme was learned from books. If one knows the rhyme from practice, the final lines have meaning; if one has read it, the final lines may seem to be an addition or a separate verse. The Munroe and Francis collections omit the final couplet. In the McLoughlin *Mother Goose's Melodies* (no date, c. 1860) they are interpreted as an independent poem and are separated from the preceding lines by a rule. In the Ashmead, Philadelphia, edition of *Mother Goose's Chimes, Rhymes, and Melodies*, however, the editors seem to have been aware of the game and rendered the last lines as

---

* Note the variant version on page 30, without the concluding couplet.

> And here comes a chopper to chop—off—
> the—last—man's—head.

Today it would seem to be solely a reading rhyme.

Publication has also resulted in a fantastic dilution of Mother Goose. It is now possible to find enormous volumes, with hundreds of rhymes ripped from all possible sources, regardless of any potential interest to the reader, simply to make a different and a bigger book. The result is a parent's book, in which the browsing parent skims through scores of verses to locate a handful of favorites.

All of these factors have resulted in a leveling, so that everything is much the same: a succession of verses, frozen in archaic language or dialect that often does not permit the metrics to succeed today; sometimes with a connected meaning, but just as often with only the limited meaning of isolated phrases. In short, Mother Goose functionally is something that the parent reads to his child, assuming it will please him, while the child in turn memorizes it and is pleased by it.

This is one aspect of the Mother Goose rhyme. The other is a collection of gorgeous images, untrammeled by distracting dances or foolish stunts; stupid rhymes and missed rhymes; subjects so idiotic as to be brilliant, and unintentional nonsense far greater than the work of the greatest nonsense poets.

New York, 1969   E. F. BLEILER

THE TRUE MOTHER GOOSE

BOSTON:
MUNROE & FRANCIS.

MOTHER GOOSE'S

M E L O D I E S.

The only Pure Edition.

CONTAINING

ALL THAT HAVE EVER COME TO LIGHT OF HER

MEMORABLE WRITINGS,

TOGETHER

WITH THOSE WHICH HAVE BEEN DISCOVERED AMONG THE MSS. OF

HERCULANEUM.

LIKEWISE

EVERY ONE RECENTLY FOUND IN THE SAME STONE BOX
WHICH HOLD THE GOLDEN PLATES OF THE BOOK OF MORMON.

THE WHOLE

COMPARED, REVISED, AND SANCTIONED,

BY ONE OF

THE ANNOTATORS OF THE GOOSE FAMILY.

WITH MANY NEW ENGRAVINGS.

Entered, according to Act of Congress, in the year 1833, by MUNROE & FRANCIS, in the Clerk's office, of the District Court of Massachusetts.

New York and Boston:
C. S. FRANCIS AND COMPANY.

HEAR WHAT MA'AM GOOSE SAYS!

My dear little Blossoms, there are now in this world, and always will be, a great many grannies besides myself, both in petticoats and pantaloons, some a deal younger to be sure; but all monstrous wise, and of my own family name. These old women, who never had chick nor child of their own, but who always know how to bring up other people's children, will tell you with very long faces, that my enchanting, quieting, soothing volume, my all-sufficient anodyne for cross, peevish, won't-be-comforted little bairns, ought to be laid aside for more learned books, such as *they* could select and publish. Fudge! I tell you that all their batterings can't deface my beauties, nor their wise pratings equal my wiser prattlings; and all imitators of my refreshing songs might as well write a new Billy Shakespeare as another Mother Goose: we two great poets were born together, and we shall go out of the world together

No, no, my Melodies will never die,
While nurses sing, or babies cry.

GOOSE'S MELODIES.

LITTLE boy blue, come blow your horn,
The sheep's in the meadow, the cow's in the corn,
What! is this the way you mind your sheep,
Under the haycock fast asleep?

There was a mad man,
　　And he had a mad wife,
And they lived all in a mad lane!
They had three children all at a birth,
And they too were mad every one.

　　The father was mad,
　　The mother was mad,
The children all mad beside;
And upon a mad horse they all of them got,
And madly away did ride.

Baa, baa, black sheep, have you any wool ?
Yes, marry have I, three bags full,
One for my master, and one for my dame,
And one for the little boy that lives in the lane.

To market, to market, to buy a penny bun,
Home again, home again, market is done.

The man in the wilderness,
Asked me,
How many strawberries
Grew in the sea?
I answered him as I thought good,
As many red herrings
As grew in the wood.

Little Robin Redbreast
Sat upon a tree,
Up went the Pussy-Cat,
And down went he;
Down came Pussy-Cat,
Away Robin ran,
Says little Robin Redbreast—
Catch me if you can.

Little Robin Redbreast jumped upon a spade,
Pussy-Cat jumped after him, and then he was afraid.
Little Robin chirped and sung, and what did Pussy say?
Pussy-Cat said Mew, mew, mew,—and Robin flew away.

Sing a song of sixpence, a bag full of rye,
Four and twenty blackbirds baked in a pie:
When the pie was opened, the birds began to sing;
And wasn't this a dainty dish to set before the king?
The king was in the parlour, counting out his money;
The queen was in the kitchen, eating bread and honey;
The maid was in the garden, hanging out the clothes;
There came a little blackbird and nipt off her nose.

Lady-bird, Lady-bird,
Fly away home,
Your house is on fire,
Your children will burn.

One, Two—buckle my shoe;
Three, Four—open the door;
Five, Six—pick up sticks;
Seven, Eight—lay them straight;
Nine, Ten—a good fat hen;
Eleven, Twelve—I hope you're well.
Thirteen, Fourteen—draw the curtain;
Fifteen, Sixteen—the maid's in the kitchen;
Seventeen, Eighteen—she's in waiting.
Nineteen Twenty—my stomach's empty.

Snail, Snail,
Come out of your hole,
Or else I'll beat you black as a coal,
Snail, Snail,
Put out your head,
Or else I'll beat you till you're dead

The man in the moon came down too soon
  To inquire the way to Norridge;
The man in the south, he burnt his mouth
  With eating cold plum-porridge.

When I was a little boy, I lived by myself,
And all the bread and cheese I got I put upon a shelf;
The rats and the mice, they made such a strife,
I was forced to go to London to buy me a wife.
The streets were so broad, and the lanes were so narrow,
I was forced to bring my wife home in a wheelbarrow;
The wheelbarrow broke, and my wife had a fall,
And down came the wheelbarrow, wife and all.

Pease porridge hot, pease porridge cold,
Pease porridge in the pot nine days old.

Can you spell that with four letters?

Yes, I can——T H A T.

Sing, Sing!——What shall I sing?
The Cat's run away with the Pudding-Bag String.

When I was a little boy, I washed my mammy's dishes,
Now I am a great boy I roll in golden riches.

BYE, Baby bunting,
 Father's gone a hunting,
Mother's gone a milking,
Sister's gone a silking,
And Brother's gone to buy a skin,
To wrap the Baby bunting in.

'TWAS once upon a time, when Jenny Wren was young,
 So daintily she danced and so prettily she sung,
Robin Redbreast lost his heart, for he was a gallant bird;
So he doffed his hat to Jenny Wren, requesting to be heard.

O, dearest Jenny Wren, if you will but be mine,
You shall feed on cherry-pie and drink new currant wine,
I'll dress you like a goldfinch or any peacock gay;
So, dearest Jen, if you'll be mine, let us appoint the day.

Jenny blushed behind her fan and thus declared her mind:
Since, dearest Bob, I love you well, I take your offer kind;
Cherry-pie is very nice and so is currant wine,
But I must wear my plain brown gown and never go too fine.

Robin Redbreast rose up early all at the break of day,
And he flew to Jenny Wren's house and sang a roundelay:
He sang of Robin Redbreast and little Jenny Wren,
And when he came unto the end he then began again.

Cushy Cow bonny, let down your milk,
And I will give you a gown of silk,
A gown of silk and a silver tee,
If you'll let down your milk to me.

There were two blind men went to see
    Two cripples run a race,
The bull did fight the humblebee,
    And scratched him in the face.

Fa, Fe, Fi, Fo, Fum!
I smell the blood of an Englishman.
Be he live or be he dead,
I'll grind his bones to make me bread.

Richard and Robin were two pretty men;
They laid abed till the clock struck ten;
Robin starts up and looks at the sky,
Oh ho! brother Richard, the sun's very high,
Do you go before with the bottle and bag,
And I'll follow after on little Jack Nag.

Round about, round about,
  Gooseberry-Pie,
My father loves good ale,
  And so do I.

We'll go to the wood, says Richard to Robin,
We'll go to the wood, says Robin to Bobin,
We'll go to the wood, says John all alone,
We'll go to the wood, says every one.

What to do there? says Richard to Robin,
What to do there? says Robin to Bobin,
What to do there? says John all alone,
What to do there? says every one.

We'll shoot at a wren, says Richard to Robin,
We'll shoot at a wren, says Robin to Bobin,
We'll shoot at a wren, says John all alone,
We'll shoot at a wren, says every one.

Then pounce, then pounce, says Richard to Robin,
Then pounce, then pounce, says Robin to Bobin,

Then pounce, then pounce, says John all alone,
Then pounce, then pounce, says every one.

She's dead, she's dead, says Richard to Robin,
She's dead, she's dead, says Robin to Bobin,
She's dead, she's dead, says John all alone,
She's dead, she's dead, says every one.

How get her home? says Richard to Robin,
How get her home? says Robin to Bobin,
How get her home? says John all alone,
How get her home? says every one.

In a cart and six horses, says Richard to Robin,
In a cart and six horses, says Robin to Bobin,
In a cart and six horses, says John all alone,
In a cart and six horses, says every one.

How shall we dress her? says Richard to Robin,
How shall we dress her? says Robin to Bobin,
How shall we dress her? says John all alone,
How shall we dress her? says every one.

We'll hire seven cooks, says Richard to Robin,
We'll hire seven cooks, says Robin to Bobin,
We'll hire seven cooks, says John all alone,
We'll hire seven cooks, says every one.

B

There was an old woman lived under the hill,
And if she's not gone she lives there still.
Baked apples she sold, and cranberry pies,
And she's the old woman that never told lies.

Shoe the colt,
Shoe the colt,
Shoe the wild mare;
Here a nail,
There a nail,
Colt must go bare.

There were two birds sat upon a stone,
> Fal de ral—al de ral—laddy.
One flew away, and then there was one,
> Fal de ral—al de ral—laddy.
The other flew after, and then there was none,
> Fal de ral—al de ral—laddy.
So the poor stone was left all alone,
> Fal de ral—al de ral—laddy.
One of these little birds back again flew,
> Fal de ral—al de ral—laddy.
The other came after, and then there were two,
> Fal de ral—al de ral—laddy.
Says one to the other, Pray how do you do,
> Fal de ral—al de ral—laddy.
Very well, thank you, and pray how are you,
> Fal de ral—al de ral—laddy.

I'll tell you a story
About Mary Morey,
And now my story's begun.
I'll tell you another
About her brother,
And now my story's done.

Nose, Nose, jolly red Nose,
And what gave you that jolly red Nose?
Nutmegs and cinnamon, spices and cloves,
And they gave me this jolly red Nose.

Sweep, sweep,
Chimney sweep,
From the bottom to the top,
Sweep all up,
Chimney sweep,
From the bottom to the top.

Climb by rope,
Or climb by ladder,
Without either
I'll climb farther.

One misty, moisty morning,
  When cloudy was the weather,
I chanced to meet an old man clothed all in leather.
He began to compliment, and I began to grin,
  How do you do, and how do you do?
  And how do you do again?

In April's sweet month,

When the leaves 'gin to spring,

Little lambs skip like fairies

And birds build and sing.

There was an old woman tost up in a blanket,
Seventy times as high as the moon,
What she did there, I cannot tell you,
But in her hand she carried a broom.
Old woman, old woman, old woman, said I,
O whither, O whither, O whither so high?
To sweep the cobwebs from the sky,
And I shall be back again by and by.

Shoe the horse, and shoe the mare,
But let the little colt go bare.

The north wind doth blow,
  And we shall have snow,
And what will poor Robin do then?
                        Poor thing!

He'll sit in the barn
  And keep himself warm,
And hide his head under his wing,
                        Poor thing!

Cold and raw the north winds blow
  Bleak in the morning early,
All the hills are covered with snow,
  And winter's now come fairly.

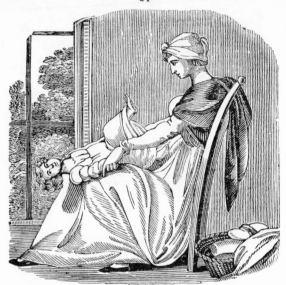

Hey, my kitten, my kitten,
    And hey my kitten my deary,
Such a sweet pet as this
    Was neither far nor neary.

Here we go up, up, up,
    And here we go down, down, downy,

Here we go backward and forward,
    And here we go round, round, roundy.

Where was a jewel and pretty,
    Where was a sugar and spicey?
Hush a bye babe in the cradle,
    And we'll go abroad in a tricey.

Did his papa torment it?
    And vex his own baby will he?
Give me a hand and I'll beat him,
    With your red coral and whistle.

Here we go up, up, up,
    And here we go down, down, downy,
And here we go backward and forward,
    And here we go round, round, roundy.

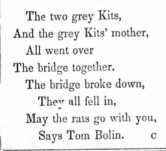

The two grey Kits,
And the grey Kits' mother,
    All went over
The bridge together.
    The bridge broke down,
        They all fell in,
May the rats go with you,
    Says Tom Bolin. c

Hark! hark! the dogs do bark,
  The beggars have come to town;
Some in rags, and some in tags,
  And some in velvet gowns.

Diddle diddle dumpling, my son John
Went to bed with his breeches on,
One stocking off, and one stocking on,
Diddle diddle dumpling, my son John.

As I was going to Derby upon a market day,
    I met the finest ram, sir, that ever fed on hay,
        On hay, on hay, on hay,
I met the finest ram, sir, that ever fed on hay.

This ram was fat behind, sir; this ram was fat before;
This ram was ten yards round, sir; indeed he was no more.
        No more, no more, no more;
This ram was ten yards round, sir; indeed he was no more.

The horns grew on his head, sir, they were so wondrous
        high,
As I've been plainly told, sir, they reached up to the sky,
        The sky, the sky, the sky,
As I've been plainly told, sir, they reached up to the sky.

The tail grew on his back, sir, was six yards and an ell,
And it was sent to Derby to toll the market bell,
        The bell, the bell, the bell;
And it was sent to Derby to toll the market bell.

Hogs in the garden, catch'em Towser;
    Cows in the corn-field, run boys, run;
Cats in the cream-pot, run girls, run girls;
Fire on the mountains, run boys, run.

The Cuckoo is a bonny bird,
   She sings as she flies,
She brings us good tidings,
   And tells us no lies.

She sucks little bird's eggs
   To make her voice clear,
And never cries Cuckoo!
   Till Spring of the year.

Lavender blue, and Rosemary green,
When I am king, you shall be queen,
Call up my maids at four of the clock,
Some to the wheel, and some to the rock,
Some to make hay, and some to shell corn,
And you and I will keep the bed warm.

The Lion and the Unicorn
   Were fighting for the crown—
The lion beat the unicorn
   All about the town.
Some gave them white bread,
   And some gave them brown,
Some gave them plum-cake,
   And sent them out of town.

Little Johnny Pringle had a little Pig,
It was very little, so was not very big.
As it was playing beneath the shed,
In half a minute poor Piggy was dead.
So Johnny Pringle he sat down and cried,
And Betty Pringle she laid down and died.
There is the history of one, two, and three,
Johnny Pringle, Betty Pringle, and Piggy Wiggie.

You owe me five shillings,
Say the bells of St. Helen's.

When will you pay me?
Say the bells of Old Bailey.

When I grow rich,
Say the bells of Shoreditch.

When will that be?
Say the bells of Stepney.

I do not know,
Says the great bell of Bow.

Two sticks in an apple,
Ring the bells of Whitechapel.

Halfpence and farthings,
Say the bells of St. Martin's.

Kettles and pans,
Say the bells of St. Ann's.

Brickbats and tiles,
Say the bells of St. Giles.

Old shoes and slippers,
Say the bells of St. Peter's.

Pokers and tongs,
Say the bells of St. John's.

Once in my life I married a wife,
   And where do you think I found her?
On Gretna Green, in velvet sheen,
   And I took up a stick to pound her,
She jumped over a barberry-bush,
   And I jump'd over a timber,
I showed her a gay gold ring,
   And she showed me her finger.

Ride a cock horse to Charing-Cross,
So see a young woman
Jump on a white horse,
With rings on her fingers
And bells on her toes,
And she shall have music
Wherever she goes.

Johnny shall have a new bonnet,
And Johnny shall go to the fair,
And Johnny shall have a blue ribbon
To tie up his bonny brown hair.

And why may not I love Johnny,
And why may not Johnny love me?
And why may not I love Johnny
As well as another body?

And here's a leg for a stocking,
And here's a foot for a shoe,
And he has a kiss for daddy,
And two for his mammy also.

And why may not I love Johnny?
And why, &c. &c.

Who comes here ?　A Grenadier,
What do you want ?　A pot of beer.
Where's your money ?　I forgot.
Get you gone, you drunken sot.

Smiling girls, rosy boys,
Come and buy my little toys,
Monkeys made of gingerbread,
And sugar horses painted red.

There was an old woman, she liv'd in a shoe,
She had so many children she didn't know what to do,
She gave them some broth without any bread,
She whipt them all soundly and put them to bed.

Heigh ding a ding, what shall I sing?
How many holes in a skimmer?
Four and twenty.   I'm half starving!
Mother, pray give me some dinner.

Hey rub-a-dub, ho rub-a-dub, three maids in a tub,
  And who do you think was there?
The butcher, the baker, the candlestick-maker,
  And all of them gone to the fair.

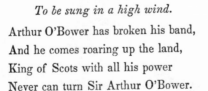

To be sung in a high wind.

Arthur O'Bower has broken his band,
And he comes roaring up the land,
King of Scots with all his power
Never can turn Sir Arthur O'Bower.

Hush-a-bye, baby, upon the tree-top,
When the wind blows the cradle will rock;
When the bough breaks the cradle will fall,
Down tumble cradle and baby and all.

Daffy-down-dilly is new come to town,
With a petticoat green, and a bright yellow gown,
And her little white blossoms are peeping around.

There was an old woman, and what do you think?
She liv'd upon nothing—but victuals and drink:
Victuals and drink were the chief of her diet,
And yet this old lady scarce ever was quiet.

The rose is red, the violet blue,
The gillyflower sweet—and so are you.
These are the words you bade me say
For a pair of new gloves on Easter-day.

Great A, little a, bouncing B,
The Cat's in the Cupboard, and she can't see.

The little black dog ran round the house,
   And set the bull a roaring,
And drove the monkey in the boat,
   Who set the oars a rowing,
And scared the cock upon the rock,
   Who crack'd his throat with crowing.

Tell tale tit,
Your tongue shall be slit,
And all the dogs in our town
Shall have a bit.

Saturday night shall be my whole care
To powder my locks and curl my hair;
On Sunday morning my love will come in,
And marry me then with a pretty gold ring.

Dear Sensibility, O la!
I heard a little lamb cry, baa!
Says I, " So you have lost mamma?"

" Baa !"

The little lamb, as I said so,
Frisking about the fields did go,
And, frisking, trod upon my toe.

" Oh !"

There was a man in our town,
  And he was wond'rous wise,
He jump'd into a bramble-bush,
  And scratch'd out both his eyes;
And when he saw his eyes were out,
  With all his might and main
He jump'd into another bush,
  And scratch'd them in again.

D

As I was going to sell my eggs,
I met a thief with bandy legs,
Bandy legs and crooked toes,
I tript up his heels and he fell on his **nose.**

Old mistress McShuttle
Lived in a coal-scuttle,
Along with her dog and her **cat;**
What they ate I can't tell,
But 'tis known very well,
That none of the party were fat.

Cock a doodle doo,
My dame has lost her shoe;
My master's lost his fiddlestick,
And knows not what to do.

There was a little man,
And he had a little gun,
And his bullets were made of lead,
He shot John Sprig
Through the middle of his wig,
And knocked it right off his head.

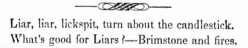

Liar, liar, lickspit, turn about the candlestick.
What's good for Liars?—Brimstone and fires.

Pussy sits behind the log,
　　How can she be fair?
Then comes in the little dog,
　　Pussy, are you there?
So, so, dear mistress Pussy,
　　Pray tell me how you do?
I thank you, little dog,
　　I'm very well just now.

How many days has my baby to play?
　　Saturday, Sunday, Monday,
　　Tuesday, Wednesday, Thursday, Friday,
　　Saturday, Sunday, Monday.

Pat a cake, pat a cake,
　　Baker's man!
So I do, master, as fast as I can.
　　Pat it, and prick it,
And mark it with T,
　　And then it will serve
For Tommy and me.

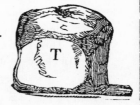

There was a man and he had naught,
　　And robbers came to rob him;
He crept up to the chimney top,
　　And then they thought they had him.
But he got down on t'other side,
　　And then they could not find him:
He ran fourteen miles in fifteen days,
　　And never look'd behind him.

Ding——dong——bell, the cat's in the well,
Who put her in? little Johnny Green.
Who pulled her out? great Johnny Stout.
What a naughty boy was that,
To drown poor pussy cat;
Who never did him any harm,
And killed the mice in his father's barn.

Lazy Tom with jacket blue,
Stole his father's gouty shoe
The worst of harm that dad can wish him,
Is his gouty shoe may fit him.

Bonny lass! bonny lass!
   Will you be mine?
You shall neither wash dishes
   Nor serve the wine,
But sit on a cushion and sew up a seam,
And you shall have strawberries, sugar, and cream.

I won't be my father's Jack,
   I won't be my father's Jill,
I will be the fiddler's wife,
   And have music when I will.
T'other little tune, t'other little tune,
Prythee, love, play me t'other little tune.

LONDON BRIDGE.

London bridge is broken down,
　　Dance over my Lady Lee,
London bridge is broken down,
　　With a gay ladye.

How shall we build it up again?
　　Dance over my Lady Lee,
How shall we build it up again?
　　With a gay ladye.

We'll build it up with gravel and stone,
　　Dance over my Lady Lee,
We'll build it up with gravel and stone,
　　With a gay ladye.

Gravel and stone will be washed away,
　　Dance over my Lady Lee,
Gravel and stone will be washed away,
　　With a gay ladye.

We'll build it up with iron and steel,
　　Dance over my Lady Lee,
We'll build it up with iron and steel,
　　With a gay ladye.

Iron and steel will bend and break,
  Dance over my Lady Lee,
Iron and steel will bend and break,
   With a gay ladye.

We'll build it up with silver and gold,
  Dance over my Lady Lee,
We'll build it up with silver and gold,
   With a gay ladye.

Silver and gold will be stolen away,
  Dance over my Lady Lee,
Silver and gold will be stolen away,
   With a gay ladye.

We'll set a man to watch it then,
  Dance over my Lady Lee,
We'll set a man to watch it then,
   With a gay ladye.

Suppose the man should fall asleep,
  Dance over my Lady Lee,
Suppose the man should fall asleep,
   With a gay ladye.

We'll put a pipe into his mouth,
  Dance over my Lady Lee,
We'll put a pipe into his mouth,
   With a gay ladye.

E

Tom, Tom, the piper's son,
Stole a pig, and away he run;
  The pig was eat,
  And Tom was beat,
And Tom ran crying down the street.

Little king Boggen he built a fine hall,
Pie-crust and pastry-crust, that was the wall;
The windows were made of black-puddings and white,
And slated with pancakes—you ne'er saw the like.

To bed, to bed, says Sleepy-Head;
    Let's stay awhile, says Slow;
Put on the pot, says Greedy-Gut,
    We'll sup before we go.

Dingty diddledy, my mammy's maid,
She stole oranges, I am afraid:
Some in her pocket, some in her sleeve,
She stole oranges, I do believe.

Ride away, ride away,
　　Johnny shall ride,
And he shall have pussy-cat
　　Tied to one side;
And he shall have little dog
　　Tied to the other,
And Johnny shall ride
　　To see his grandmother.

Hush-a-bye, baby, lie still with thy daddy,
　　Thy mammy is gone to the mill,
To get some meal to bake a cake;
　　So pray, my dear baby, lie still.

Little lad, little lad,
　　Where were you born?
Far off in Lancashire, under a thorn,
　　Where they sup butter-milk
　　With a ram's horn;
And a pumpkin scoop'd,
　　With a yellow rim,
Is the bonny bowl they breakfast in.

Pretty John Watts,
We are troubled with rats,
Will you drive them out of the house?
We have mice too in plenty,
That feast in the pantry,
But let them stay and nibble away,
What harm in a little brown mouse?

Shake a leg, wag a leg, when will you gang?
At midsummer, mother, when the days are lang.

See saw, sacradown, sacradown,
Which is the way to Boston town?
One foot up, the other foot down,
That is the way to Boston town.
Boston town's changed into a city
But I've no room to change my ditty.

Hop away, skip away, my baby wants to play.
My baby wants to play every day.

Bobby Shaftoe's gone to sea,
Silver buckles on his knee;
He'll come back and marry me,
       Pretty Bobby Shaftoe.

Bobby Shaftoe's fat and fair,
Combing down his yellow hair,
He's my love forevermore,
       Pretty Bobby Shaftoe.

Pussy cat, pussy cat, where have you been?
I've been to London to see the Queen.
Pussy cat, pussy cat, what did you there?
I frightened a little mouse under the chair.

Taffy was a Welchman, Taffy was a thief,
Taffy came to my house and stole a piece of beef;
I went to Taffy's house, Taffy wan't at home,
Taffy came to my house and stole a marrow-bone;
I went to Taffy's house, Taffy was in bed,
I took the marrow-bone, and beat about his head.

Boys and girls, come out to play,
The moon does shine as bright as day,
Leave your supper, and leave your sleep,
And meet your playfellows in the street;
Come with a whoop, and come with a call
And come with a good will, or not at all.
Up the ladder and down the wall,
A halfpenny roll will serve us all.
You find milk and I'll find flour,
And we'll have pudding in half an hour.

Go to bed, Tom, go to bed, Tom—
Merry or sober, go to bed, Tom.

Ride a cock horse to Banbury-cross
    To see what Tommy can buy ;
A penny white loaf, a penny white cake,
    And a two penny apple-pie.

Ride a cock horse to Shrewsbury-cross,
To buy little Johnny a galloping horse :
It trots behind and it ambles before,
And Johnny shall ride till he can ride no more.

Jemmy Jed went into a shed,
And made of a ted of straw his bed;
An owl came out and flew about,
And Jemmy Jed up stakes and fled.
Wan't Jemmy Jed a staring fool,
Born in the woods to be scar'd by an owl?

How many miles to Babylon?
Threescore miles and ten.
Can I get there by candle-light?
Yes, and back again.

Rock-a-bye, baby,
Your cradle is green,
Father's a nobleman,
Mother's a queen,
And Betty's a lady,
And wears a gold ring,
And Johnny's a drummer,
And drums for the king.

Trip upon trenchers,
And dance upon dishes,
My mother sent me for yeast, some yeast,
She bid me tread lightly,
And come again quickly,
For fear the young men would play me some jest.

Yet didn't you see, yet didn't you see,
What naughty tricks they put upon me?
They broke my pitcher, and spilt my water,
And huff'd my mother, and chid her daughter.
And kissed my sister instead of me.

What's the news of the day,
Good neighbour, I pray?
They say the balloon
Has gone up to the moon.

There was an old man in a velvet coat,
He kiss'd a maid and gave her a groat;
The groat was crack'd and would not go.
Ah, old man, do you serve me so?

Three wise men of Gotham
Went to sea in a bowl
And if the bowl had been stronger
My song had been longer.

Wash me and comb me
And lay me down softly,
And set me on a bank to dry,
That I may look pretty,
When some one comes by.

Up in the green orchard there is a green tree,
The finest of pippins that ever you see ;
The apples are ripe, and ready to fall,
And Reuben and Robin shall gather them all.

Harry cum Parry, when will you marry ?
  When apples and pears are ripe.
I'll come to your wedding without any bidding,
  And stay with the bride all night.

I will sing you a song
Of the days that are long,
Of the woodcock and the sparrow,
Of the little dog that burnt his tail,
And she shall be whipt to-morrow.

Jog on, jog on, the footpath way,
And merrily jump the style, boys,
A merry heart goes all the day,
Your sad one tires in a mile, boys.

I had a little Doll,
  The prettiest ever seen,
She washed me the dishes,
  And kept the house clean.
She went to the mill
  To fetch me some flour,
And always got it home
  In less than an hour;
She baked me my bread,
  She brewed me my ale,
She sat by the fire
  And told many a fine tale.

When I was a little he,
My mother took me on her knee,
Smiles and kisses gave with joy,
And call'd me oft her darling boy.

F

Is master Smith within?—Yes, that he is.
Can he set a shoe?—Ay, marry, two
Here a nail, and there a nail,
Tick—tack—too.

Charley loves good cake and ale,
Charley loves good candy,
Charley loves to kiss the girls,
When they are clean and handy.

John O'Gudgeon he was a wild man,
He whipt his children now and then,
When he whipt them, he made them dance,
Out of Ireland into France.

Peter, Peter, pumpkin eater,
Had a wife and couldn't keep her;
He put her in a pumpkin shell,
And then he kept her very well.
Peter, Peter, pumpkin eater,
Had another and didn't love her;
Peter learnt to read and spell,
And then he loved her very well.

Jack and Jill went up the hill
To draw a pail of water;
Jack fell down and broke his crown,
And Jill came tumbling after.

There was an old man, and he had a calf,
And that's half;
He took him out of the stall and put him on the wall,
And that's all.

Goosey, goosey, gander, where dost thou wander?

Up stairs and down stairs, and in my lady's chamber;

There I met an old man that would not say his prayers,

I took him by his hind legs and threw him down stairs.

The girl in the lane,

That couldn't speak plain,

   Cried, Gobble, gobble, gobble;

The man on the hill,

That couldn't stand still,

   Went hobble, hobble, hobble.

Robert Barns, fellow fine,
Can you shoe this horse of mine,
So that I may cut a shine?
    Yes, good sir, and that I can,
    As well as any other man;
There a nail, and here a prod,
And now, good sir, your horse is shod.

Hey ding a ding, ding, I heard a bird sing,
The parliament soldiers are gone to the king.

Pibroch of Donnel Dhu,
    Pibroch of Donnel,
Wake thy voice anew,
    Summon Clan-Connel.
Come away, come away,
    Hark to the summons,
Come in your war array,
    Gentles and commons!

Come as the winds come,
    When forests are rended,
Come as the waves come,
    When navies are stranded.
Faster come, faster come, faster and faster,
    Chief, vassal, page and groom,
        Tenant and master!

Fast they come, fast they come,
    See how they gather!
Wide waves the eagle plume blended with heather.
    Cast your plaids, draw your blades,
        Forward each man set!
Pibroch of Donnel Dhu, now for the onset!

Jack Sprat could eat no fat;
  His wife could eat no lean;
So 'twixt them both they cleared the cloth,
  And lick'd the platter clean.

There was a little boy went into a barn,
  And lay down on some hay;
A calf came out and smelt about,
  And the little boy ran away.

The sow came in with the saddle,

The little pig rock'd the cradle,

The dish jump'd up on the table

To see the pot swallow the ladle.

The spit that stood behind the door

Threw the pudding-stick on the floor.

Odsplut! said the gridiron,

Can't you agree?

I'm the head constable,

Bring them to me.

G

Little Tommy Tucker, sing for your supper:
What shall I sing? white bread and butter.
How shall I cut it without any knife?
How shall I marry without any wife?

I would, if I could;
If I couldn't, how could I?
I couldn't without I could, could I?
Could you without you could, could ye?
Could ye, could ye?
You couldn't, without you could, could ye?

Hiccory, diccory, dock,
The mouse run up the clock;
The clock struck one, and down he run,
Hiccory, diccory, dock.

Jacky, come give me your fiddle,
　If ever you mean to thrive.
Nay, I'll not give my fiddle
　To any man alive.

If I should give my fiddle,
　They'll think that I'm gone mad,
For many a joyful day
　My fiddle and I have had.

There was a Piper had a Cow,
    And he had naught to give her,
He pull'd out his pipes and play'd her a tune,
    And bade the cow consider.

    The cow considered very well,
        And gave the piper a penny,
        And bade him play the other tune,
        " Corn rigs are bonny."

Away, pretty robin, fly home to your nest,
To make you my captive I still should like best,
    And feed you with worms and with bread :
Your eyes are so sparkling, your feathers so soft,
Your little wings flutter so pretty aloft,
    And your breast is all cover'd with red.

    Handy-spandy, Jacky dandy,
    Loves plum-cake and sugar candy.
    He bought some at a grocer's shop,
And pleased away went hop, hop, hop.

When good King Arthur ruled his land
   He was a goodly king;
He stole three pecks of barley meal
   To make a bag-pudding.
A bag-pudding the king did make,
   And stuff'd it well with plums;
And in it put great lumps of fat,
   As big as my two thumbs.
The king and queen did eat thereof,
   And noblemen beside;
And what they could not eat that night,
   The queen next morning fried.

Bow, wow, wow,
    Whose dog art thou ?
Little Tom Tinker's dog,
    Whose dog art thou ?

See saw, Jack-a-daw,
Johnny shall have a new master ;
Johnny shall have but a penny a day,
Because he can work no faster.

We're three brethren out of Spain,
Come to court your daughter Jane.
My daughter Jane she is too young,
She has no skill in a flattering tongue.
Be she young or be she old,
It's for her gold she must be sold
So fare you well, my lady gay,
We shall return another day.

Mistress Mary, quite contrary,
    How does your garden grow?
With silver bells and cockle shells,
    And maidens all a row.

When I was a little boy, my mother kept me in,
Now I am a great boy, and fit to serve the king;
I can handle a musket, I can smoke a pipe,
I can kiss a pretty girl at ten o'clock at night.

Mary had a pretty bird,
    Feathers bright and yellow,
Slender legs, upon my word
    He was a pretty fellow.

The sweetest notes he always sung,
    Which much delighted Mary
And often where the cage was hung,
    She stood to hear Canary.

Rigadoon, rigadoon, now let him fly.
Sit upon mother's foot, jump him up high.

One,
Two,
Three,
Four,
Five,
I caught a hare alive.
Six,
Seven,
Eight,
Nine,
Ten,
I let her go again.

Tom, Tom, of Islington,
Married a wife on Sunday,
Bro't her home on Monday,
Hired a house on Tuesday,
Fed her well on Wednesday,
Sick was she on Thursday,
Dead was she on Friday,
Sad was Tom on Saturday,
To bury his wife on Sunday.

I had a little husband no bigger than my thumb,
I put him in a pint pot, and there I bid him drum;
I bought a little handkerchief to wipe his little nose,
And a pair of little garters to tie his little hose.

As I was going to St. Ives,
I met seven wives,
Every wife had seven sacks,
Every sack had seven cats,
Every cat had seven kits.
Kits, cats, sacks and wives,
How many were going to St. Ives?

Miss Jane had a bag, and a mouse was in it,
  She opened the bag, he was out in a minute;
The Cat saw him jump, and run under the table,
And the dog said, catch him, puss, soon as you're able.

Cross Patch, draw the latch,
  Sit by the fire and spin;
Take a cup, and drink it up,
  Then call your neighbours in.

See-saw, Margery Daw,
Sold her bed, and lay upon straw.
Was not she a dirty slut,
To sell her bed and lay in the dirt?

What care I how black I be?
Twenty pounds will marry me.
If twenty won't, forty shall,
I'm my mother's bouncing girl.

Here's A, B, C, D, E, F and G,
H, I, J, K, L, M, N, O, and P,
Q, R, S, T, U, V, W, X, Y, and Z;
And here is good mamma, who knows
This is the fount whence learning flows.

———⟨≈≈≈⟩———

Milk-man, milk-man, where have you been?
In Buttermilk channel up to my chin,
    I spilt my milk, and I spoilt my clothes,
    And got a long icicle hung to my nose.

There was an old woman
    Sold puddings and pies,
She went to the mill,
    And the dust flew in her eyes.
  While through the streets
  To all she meets,
    She ever cries,
    Hot Pies—Hot Pies.

A cow and a calf,
  An ox and a half,
Forty good shillings and three,
 Is not that enough tocher
 For a shoemaker's daughter,
  A bonny sweet lass
  With a coal-black ee?

The little Robin grieves
    When the snow is on the ground,
For the trees have no leaves,
    And no berries can be found.

The air is cold, the worms are hid,
    For Robin here what can be done?
Let's strow around some crums of bread,
    And then he'll live till snow is gone.

Little Jack Nory
Told me a story
How he tried
Cock-horse to ride,
Sword and scabbard
by his side,
Saddle, leaden spurs
and switches,
His pocket tight
With cents all bright,
Marbles, tops, puzzles, props,
Now he's put in jacket and breeches.

There were two blackbirds sitting on a hill,
One name Jack, and the other name Jill;
Fly away, Jack,—fly away, Jill,
Come again, Jack,—come again, Jill.

Willy boy, Willy boy, where are you going?
    O let me go with you this sunshiny day.
I'm going to the meadow to see them a mowing,
    I'm going to help the girls turn the new hay.

Fee, Faw, Foe, Fum,
    I smell the blood of an Englishman,
    Dead or alive, I will have some

A was an Angler, went out in a fog,
  Who fished all the day and caught only a frog.

B was cook Betty, she's baking a pie,
  With ten or twelve apples all piled up on high.

C was a Custard cast in a glass dish,
  And has in it cinnamon much as you wish.

D was fat Dick, who did nothing but eat,
  He would leave book and slate for a nice piece of meat.

E is an Egg, in a basket with more,
  Which Peggy will sell for a shilling a score.

F is a Fiddler, very fine I declare,
  He makes pretty music with catgut and hair.

G was a Greyhound as fleet as the wind;
  In the race or the course left all others behind.

H was a Heron who lived near a pond,
  Of gobbling up fish he was wondrously fond.

I was the Ice on which Billy would skate,
  So up went his heels and down went his pate.

J was Joe Jenkins who played on the fiddle;
  He began twenty tunes and left off in the middle.

K was a Kitten who jumped at a cork,
  And learnt to eat mice without knife or fork.

is a Lark who sings us a song,
  And wakes us betimes, lest we sleep too long.

was Miss Molly who turned in her toes
  And hung down her head till her knees touched her nose.

was a Nosegay sprinkled with dew,
  Pulled in the morning and given to you.

was an Owl who looks marvellous wise,
  But he's watching a mouse with his large round eyes.

is a Parrot with feathers like gold,
  Who talks just as much and no more than he's told.

is the Queen that governs England,
  And sets on a throne very lofty and grand.

is a Raven perched up in an oak,
  And with a gruff voice cries croak, croak, croak.

is a Stork with a very long bill,
  Who swallows down fishes and frogs to his fill.

is a Trumpeter blowing his horn,
  Who tells all the news as we rise in the morn.

is a Unicorn who, as is said,
  Wears an ivory bodkin in his forehead.

is a Vulture who eats a great deal,
  Devouring a dog or cat at a meal.

W was a Watchman who guarded the street,
  Lest robbers or thieves the people should meet.

X was king Xerxes, who, if you don't know,
  He reigned over Persia a great while ago.

Y is the Year that is passing away,
  And still growing shorter every day.

Z is a Zebra whom you've heard of before ;—
  So here ends my rhyme till I find you some more.

A FARMER went trotting upon his grey mare,
        Bumpety bumpety bump,
With his daughter behind him so rosy and fair,
        Lumpety lumpety lump.

A raven cried croak, and they all tumbled down,
        Bumpety bumpety bump ;
The mare broke her knees and the farmer his crown,
        Lumpety lumpety lump.

The mischievous raven flew laughing away,
        Bumpety bumpety bump,
And vowed he would serve them the same next day,
        Lumpety lumpety lump.

A BIBLIOGRAPHIC NOTE

FOR SPECIALISTS

Although the bibliography of Mother Goose in America has been seriously studied for almost one hundred years, not much is definitely known about it. This is particularly true of the various Munroe and Francis Mother Goose books, which have proved to be unexpectedly complex in their publication history. While enough copies have survived to show that their printings are not simple, not enough have come down to us to permit a satisfactory classification. It is no great exaggeration to say that each new copy examined adds further confusion.

Rarity has been a great problem with all the Munroe and Francis Mother Goose books. *Mother Goose's Quarto* survives in a single copy, dated by its juvenile owner "in the year 1827." *Chimes, Rhymes, and Jingles*, registered for copyright in 1845, is known to exist in two copies in the possession of public libraries. The earliest version of *Mother Goose's Melodies* is recorded with three copies; a possible fourth has not yet been traced. There may be six copies of later versions in public libraries, and possibly an equal number lying inaccessible in private collections. Bibliographic records, too, are not always helpful. The earlier bibliographers did not recognize the importance of internal variation from copy to copy, and as a rule did not describe books fully enough to ensure identification. As a result bibliographic work must be based as much on speculation as on exact record.

Mother Goose's Melodies, the second Munroe and Francis collection, is often described as the second edition of the *Quarto*. This is not correct. It differs in contents and pagination, as well as in title, from the *Quarto*, and by publishing standards it should be considered a separate book.

Mother Goose's Melodies went through several editions, each somewhat different from the others. Two basic families of editions are involved, with a total of five states of the text. At least eight printings were involved; others almost certainly will be identified as additional copies are located. The following analysis does not pretend to be final.

Since other states will probably be discovered, it seemed unwise to use letters or numerals as designations. Instead, the name of the individual first concerned with the edition, or the library where it was first located, has been used.

Two miscellaneous points should be made. All known copies of this book bear on the title page the notice: "Entered according to Act of Congress, in the year 1833, by Munroe and Francis, in the Clerk's Office of the District Court of Massachusetts." This notice, which has caused considerable confusion, does not refer to the year in which the individual book was printed, but is simply the record of the original copyright. It appears on reprints published well into the 1860's. Secondly, for purposes of convenience, the Dover copy, reproduced in this book, has been used as the basic copy against which others are compared.

FAMILY ONE

Family One is characterized by a political preface, obviously aimed at Andrew Jackson, and an extended note signed Gilbert Gosling, both omitted from Family Two printings. Verses are arranged differently and there are several textual variations from Family Two. Family One contains two known printings, Hamilton 690 and Rosenbach 801.

HAMILTON 690 STATE

(Hamilton Collection, Princeton University Library). Since this is probably a unique copy, a collation and extracts are given.

No wrappers.   4¾″ x 5½″.   48 leaves.

[1] Blank.

[2] Same cut and text as in the Dover edition, p. [2], with slight textual differences: *Willy Shakespeare* instead of *Billy Shakespeare*, *We shall go off together*, instead of *We shall go out of the world together*.

[3] Title page. Same text; very similar typographical style to the Dover title page, but the imprint is *Boston: Printed and*

*published by Munroe and Francis, 128 Washington-Street; and
C. S. Francis, New-York.* The phrase *in the year 1833* is not set
off in commas.

[4] FAMILY DEDICATION.   *To His Excellency
The Greatest and best* GANDER *in the Country;
To his* CABINET, *that roast our family so nicely;
And to my large* FLOCK *of Cousins throughout the Union;-
To all Fellows of all Antiquarian, Scientific,
Philosophical, Etymological, Explanatory, Critical, Comical,
And every other learned and unlearned Institution;
And last, though not least,
To all worthy Members of Household Nursery Societies,
Who try to keep peace among little Nullifiers,
That are always "up in arms,"
*THIS ONLY PURE EDITION OF MOTHER GOOSE,
Undertaken as an humble attempt to illustrate and preserve
In their primitive purity, the true readings of ancient Song,
On whose Pedestal modern Melody and Metre
are triumphantly reared,
Hoping that its executions, both graphic and typographic,
will meet with approbation and applause,
Is, with most devout deference, Dedicated,
by their, and their young progeny's profound admirer,
and lineal descendant of the fair Author,*

Gilbert Gosling

[5] to 93.   The nursery rhymes. If the page is considered as
the unit of reference, approximately two-thirds of the pages
are the same as in the Dover copy, although often in very
different order. The verses on the remaining third of the pages
are scattered about differently than in the Dover copy.

94.   Tommy's Opinion of Mother Goose.

*A four-year old boy, and I know him quite well,
He wished to peruse Mother Goose for a spell,
    But his own mother said fie, fie, boy:*

Here's nice catechisms, primers, hymn-books and so,
All written by Emerson, Worcester, and co.
    Don't read that nonsensical fry, boy.

*Besides too, here's aunty's New Goosey-Book, dear,**
For musical charming it has no compeer,
    With its "radener, tadorer, tan do ree too."
You may read her unvulgar and moral-sense book,
For Goose's effects are all clean away shook,
'Twill be noticed, I hope in the next Mother's Book,
    With its 'Ringely, ringely, dahre roo noo,'
And its 'Troliloli lo loo, its troliloli lo loo.'

---

* If Tommy's mother does not here refer to E.L.F.'s Little Songs
for Little Children, recently graduated at Cambridge, I don't know
what she means. G.G.

Tommy Answers:—

"I don't want to read how a hen has two legs,
About Time how he flies, and a Beggar who begs,
    Or a Text, with a chapter and verse to it;
I learn these in school and I say them to you,
I want to read nonsense a minute or two.
    I'll promise to act none the worse for't.

You redde it yourself, ma', to Charles and to Jane,
It kept them both quiet when they were in pain,
    And you said there was nothing like Goose,
And grandma' repeats it and knows every rhyme,
And nurse has amused Tommy many a time,
    What now is the matter with Goose?

I think that the whole of the above poem is an
interpolation, although it was recently found among

many others of my venerable ancestor's papers; but it is best to insert it, on the same ground that some of the disputed dramas of Shakespeare were inserted among his genuine works, namely, there are many things in it worthy such a writer. And here I must take infinite credit to myself for my indefatigable labour in hunting out and bringing to light many lost gems, which would never have sparkled at this day nor been the cause of sparkling in others, but for me. I thought I had heretofore done all that man could do, and, for the first time, dignified my researches with the name of Quarto; yes "Mother Goose's Quarto!" but this was full of Imperfections, and to mortify me still more repeated spurious editions were thrust out in the city of New York with a King's stamp upon them, in defiance of my just rights, a shame to all correct readers, and giving worthless food to all motherly receivers to feed their babes upon. But I now resign, renounce, and utterly excommunicate said Quarto, and recommend this original, unexpurgated, restored and only pure edition, called "Mother Goose's Melodies," to musical notice and patronage, it being printed exclusively by my publishers. Respectfully. GILBERT GOSLING

[96] [cut showing a nurse, Mother Goose, holding children]

> Here's a lady so gay, singing away,
>   A parcel of children around her,
> The boys and girls all wish her to stay,
>   And they utterly tease and confound her,
> But every rhyme she had said with a chime,
> And got she has on the last page, lads,
> So close up the leaf, and put away grief,
> She'll sing them again, I'll engage, lads.

THE END

The Hamilton 690 state contains the following verses not in the Dover state: "Song set to five fingers" ("This little pig went to market, this little pig staid at home"; "This little pig had a bit of bread and butter," etc.); "Song set to five toes" ("'Let us go to the wood,' says this pig," etc.); "Bless you, bless you, Burney Bee" (two different versions); "Robin O'Bobin, the big-bellied Hen, ate more victuals than three-score men"; "When I was a little boy, I had but little wit"; "Rain, Rain, go away"; "High, diddle diddle, the Cat and the Fiddle"; "Little Miss Muffett, she sat on a tuffet"; "I had a little hobby-horse, and it was dapple-grey"; "Five children playing on the ice all on a summer's day"; "Little Jack Horner sat in a corner"; "Come listen, my boys, sit still and be mum, I'll read the apparel of Master Tom Thumb."

Several of the individual poems show variations from the Dover text.

> There was an old woman lived under the hill,
> And if she's not gone she lives there still.
> She sold apples, and she sold pies,
> And she's the old woman, that never told lies.

> Shoe the colt, Shoe the colt, Shoe the wild mare;
> Here a nail, There a nail, Yet the little colt goes bare.

> In the month of sweet April
> When the leaves begin to spring,
> Little lambs do skip like fairies
> Birds do couple, build and sing.

> There was an old woman tost up in a blanket,
> Seventeen times as high as the moon,
> What she did there no mortal can tell,
> But under her arm she carried a broom.   etc.

Omitted from "You owe me five shilling":

> When I grow rich, Say the bells of Shoreditch

> Little Robin Red-breast grieves
>   When the snow is on the ground,   etc.

With the exception of an occasional orthographic change, the remaining texts are identical with those in the Dover edition.

Three miscellaneous points should be mentioned about Hamilton 690. The cut associated with "Hush-a-bye, baby" is printed upside down; it can be seen in trimmed form, right side up, on page 36 of this Dover reprint. On page 11 the word "jolly" is misspelled as "joly," while in "The Lion and the Unicorn" an extra word "all" has been printed: "All all about the town."

There is no reason to think that Hamilton 690 should be dated any later than 1833, even though the consensus until now has been that it dates from 1835. The political dedication to President Jackson and his cabinet would fall naturally into 1833, since the events took place in the fall of 1832. It is reasonable that a book reprinted in 1835 might retain such material, much less reasonable that it should first print it. Another indication of date is to be found in G.G.'s reference to Eliza L. Follen's *Little Songs for Little Boys and Girls* as being "recently graduated at Cambridge." Mrs. Follen's book was printed in December, 1832 (*American Monthly Review* notice, January, 1833). In copies of Family One, the cut for "Dear Sensibility" (changed for later printings) contains the numerals 33, which are presumably a date. And the *American Monthly Review* for February, 1833, lists as having been published in January, 1833, a Munroe and Francis *Mother Goose's Melodies, a new edition.*

ROSENBACH 801 STATE

First described, though very ambiguously, in *Early American Children's Books* by A. S. W. Rosenbach (Southworth Press, Portland, Maine, 1933, pp. 282 ff.). In title page and text this state is the same as Hamilton 690, although the typographical errors on page 11 ("joly") and 13 ("all all") have been corrected. The cut for "Hush-a-bye, baby" (page 36) is still printed upside down. Illustration is identical. The publisher's imprint on the title page is: BOSTON:/ PRINTED AND PUBLISHED BY / MUNROE AND FRANCIS. / 128 WASHINGTON-STREET—AND C. S. FRANCIS, NEW-

YORK. The wrapper may be of interest since it is not adequately described elsewhere. [i] GOOSE'S MELODIES. / THE ONLY PURE EDITION./ [cut of old woman in shoe from page 36 (Dover reprint)] BOSTON: / MUNROE & FRANCIS, 128 WASHINGTON-STREET; / CHARLES S. FRANCIS, NEW-YORK. All in double box. [ii] Blank. [iii] Blank. [iv] GOOSE'S MELODIES. / THE / ONLY PURE EDITION./ [cut of Jack and Jill from page 70 (Dover reprint)] BOSTON:/ MUNROE & FRANCIS, 128 Washington-Street. / rule/ 1835. All in double box.

A curious problem has arisen with the Rosenbach state. Rosenbach's copy and the Boston Public Library copy both lack pages [1] and [2], present in Hamilton 690. This includes the second dedication page.

FAMILY TWO

Four other versions of *Mother Goose's Melodies* are known, all of which are closely related in general contents, illustration, page placement, textual details of individual verses, and even small points of physical typography. They all differ from Family One. In general the Dover state, which seems to be second in chronological order, is typical of members of Family Two.

For the earliest state of Family Two (the Brown University copy) *Mother Goose's Melodies* has been completely reset typographically, although the printing style, where other factors have not interfered, is very close to that of Hamilton 690. This same typography was used through the succession of editions that followed, indicating that lock-ups (or stereo plates on occasion) must have been stored at the plant between printings. This physical type shows a gradual deterioration from printing to printing, with an increasing number of broken letters, mashed rules and evidences of worn type. Indeed, it is not an exaggeration to say that the chain of editions can be traced through type as well as through textual changes. For example, on page 11 (in this Dover reprint), the dot is missing on the second "sing" in "Sing, Sing." This dot continues to be missing in later reprints. In the Brown state of Family Two, which is otherwise demonstrably earlier, this dot is present. Many other specific examples of type decay could be cited.

When Munroe and Francis revised *Mother Goose's Melodies* into the Family Two text, they made many changes involving selection of verses, texts printed, and, as has been indicated above, arrangement of contents in the book. Most significant of all were changes in illustration. While a few spot illustrations were dropped, a series of cuts by the well-known New York engraver Dr. Alexander Anderson were added. Cuts with his initials AA are to be found on pages 14, 15, 21, 22, 31, 41, 45, 76, 77 and 79, while others in similar style may be attributed to him. For "Peter, Peter pumpkin eater," "The Girl in the lane," and "We're three brethren out of Spain," three new Empire-style cuts have been added. Many of the cuts in Hamilton 690, which were originally squared or lozenged, were trimmed down, presumably because of damage or wear: pages 11, 13, 24, 36, 37, 58, 82, 86 of the Dover reprint. This phenomenon, of course, demonstrates conclusively the priority of Family One copies.

A few special points may be cited to afford easy comparison with other printings: illustrations signed AB (Abel Bowen) are to be found on pages 2, 7, 9, 53, 64 and perhaps 56; illustrations signed Childs (Shubael Childs or Benjamin Childs, his brother) on pages 11 and 13, and perhaps 5 and 24; illustrations signed ND (usually considered Nathaniel Dearborn, although possibly Nicholas Devereux) on the cover and pages 26 and 92; H (A. Hartwell or J. H. Hall) on pages 66 and 82.

It should be mentioned, with these initials and attributions, that a woodblock, especially when it is worn, does not always give uniform impressions. Some printings will reveal more fine lines than others, showing a signature where other impressions show a smudge. These readings have been based on several copies, in addition to the Duyckinck reproduction of Anderson's cuts.

At present four different versions (with subsidiaries) are known within Family Two. In probable chronological order these are the Brown state; the Dover state; the Whitmore state; and the Hislop state. These states differ only slightly from one another, mostly in page placement. Why the house of Munroe and Francis shifted pages (otherwise unaltered) so much from one edition to another is inexplicable, since the changes have no technological significance and make no difference editorially.

B R O W N   S T A T E

This probably unique copy is preserved in imperfect condition in Brown University Library, Providence, Rhode Island. The front wrapper and pages 1 through 4 are missing. It is remarkable in being a bridge between the earlier Hamilton 690 printing and later printings of Family Two; yet it is clearly a member of Family Two.

The Brown copy is identical in contents, illustration, and page arrangement with the Dover state, except for a few pages. Page 12 contains "High diddle diddle, the Cat and the Fiddle," and "Little Jack Horner." Page [27] contains "Song set to Five Fingers," "Song set to Five Toes," and "Bless you, bless you, Burney Bee." Page 33 contains "I had a little hobby-horse" and "Robin O'Bobin, the big-bellied Hen." Page 40 contains "When I was a little boy, I had but little wit"; "Rain, rain, go away"; and "Bye, Baby bunting." Page 54 contains "Little Miss Muffet" and "Hogs in the garden." Page 75 contains "Five children playing on the ice." All these pages contain the same cuts as Hamilton 690. On page 93 is to be found "Dear Sensibility"; on page 94, "See saw, sacradown, sacradown" and "Hop away, skip away"; on page 95 "Who comes here? A Grenadier" and "Smiling girls, rosy boys"; on page 96 "Hiccory, diccory, dock." These pages contain illustrations as in the Dover state.

It will be observed that "Jenny Wren," "As I was going to Derby," and "A was an Angler" are not included, nor is the advertisement on page 96 for *Chimes, Rhymes, and Jingles*.

The rear wrapper of the Brown copy is preserved. Page [iii] is blank, while page [iv] contains the cat and dog illustration from page 44, surrounded by a border formed of blocks of acanthus leaves and grapes. The text reads: MOTHER / GOOSE'S MELODIES. / COMPLETE./ [rule] O. P. EDITION. / [cut] BOSTON: / JOSEPH H. FRANCIS AND / C. S. FRANCIS, NEW YORK. Since the paper is very worn, punctuation is not completely clear.

It is not possible to give an exact date to this printing, but it is reasonable to assign it to the late 1830's. 1837 seems a valid hovering date.

DOVER STATE

This is the text used in this reprint. Judging from the number of surviving copies, this would seem to be the version that received widest circulation, going through several printings. Two copies of this state have been examined, as well as two separate printings for the New York distributor, C. S. Francis, and a colored clothbound copy.

These New York variants are almost identical with the Dover copy reprinted here. There are, however, a few differences in matters other than text and illustration: on pages 49 and 65, where the Dover copy has as signature marks E and F, the New York variants have D and E respectively. On the title page the publisher is given as   Boston: Printed and published by Munroe and Francis.   On page 9 of one copy, there is a typographical error: the letter "r" has dropped out of the word "inquire." These differences would indicate that stereo plates were not used, but that page lock-up differed between Boston and New York printings, possibly for a different press.

The wrappers of the New York variants differ from the wrapper for the Dover copy. They are printed on light green paper (the Dover copy is on light yellow), and the publisher is cited as C. S. Francis, New York. Note that this is not C. S. Francis and Co. The rear wrapper is decorated with a frame. In one copy this frame consists of repeated floral blocks; centered in them is the Anderson cut of "One misty, moisty morning." In the second copy, this frame consists of a series of interlocked concentric circles, with the cut from "There was a mad man." In this version the title is given as *Mother Goose's Melodeis* [sic].

A clothbound, hand-colored version of the Dover state was also sold for 25 cents. It is exactly the same internally as the Dover copy reprinted here, but the type is considerably more worn, presumably indicating a late printing within the series.

The cloth is dark brown, with MOTHER GOOSE'S MELODIES stamped in gold across the middle; this is enclosed in an impressed frame consisting of a curved "Gothic" design in double lines. The cloth is attached to the sheets by cream endpapers, with an extra lining sheet at front and rear.

Red, blue, light green, yellow and orange water colors were applied rather crudely to the illustrations, some color to each page. There is no indication of a stencil. Since there is occasional transfer of colors, the colorist probably painted bound books rather than loose sheets.

WHITMORE STATE

In his *Original Mother Goose's Melody* (Albany, 1889) William Whitmore was primarily concerned with the Isaiah Thomas *Mother Goose's Melody* and the Munroe and Francis *Mother Goose's Quarto*. Indirectly, however, he collated by comparison a copy of *Mother Goose's Melodies*, and it is possible to work backward from his data to establish a version of this book different in some respects from other copies.

The title page [1] is reproduced by Whitmore, as is page 96, the advertisement for *Chimes, Rhymes, and Jingles*. Both are identical with the corresponding pages in the Dover copy.

The individual verses seem to be the same as those in the Dover state, but not always in the same page order. On page 3 the Whitmore copy has "The North wind doth blow"; on page 23, "Shoe the horse and shoe the mare"; on page 40, "Pease porridge hot"; on page 64, "See, saw, sacradown, sacradown," etc. There are a fair number of such differences.

Whitmore does not mention "Wee Willie Winkie," "Three Little Kittens," or "Hen, hen, hen," which are characteristic of the Hislop state.

Whitmore was the first to identify certain of the artists who illustrated *Mother Goose's Melodies*: Abel Bowen, Nathaniel Dearborn (signed as ND), "Chicket" (a misreading for Childs), but he does not mention Avery, who is present with two clearly signed cuts in the Hislop state. Since Whitmore was a close and accurate collator, we may assume that Avery's work was not present.

The Whitmore state seems to be transitional between the Dover and the Hislop states. It has not been available for examination.

HISLOP STATE

This is the last of the Munroe and Francis versions of *Mother Goose's Melodies*; in turn, it served as the basis for many reprint editions by other publishers, some apparently legitimate, others apparently not. While it is closely related to the Dover state, there are a considerable number of minor changes. It does not seem necessary to detail these changes, since the first 92 pages have been reproduced in the 1905 facsimile (see below) and are readily available in most large libraries. To mention only a few details: New or additional cuts have been printed on pages 5, 10, 12, 35, 39, 40, 43, 54, 57, 58, 63, 68, 74, 78, 80, 83, 84, 88, 93. These cuts are unsigned, except for those on pages 54 and 58, which are clearly marked Avery. A few new verses have been added: "Oh, what a sweet little white mouse" (page 29), "My little pink" (page 39), "Hen, cock, cock,

cock, cock" (page 43), "Tom Brown's two little Indian boys" (page 54), "Oh, I am so happy" (page 60), "This is the way the ladies ride" (page 83), a new verse to "Willie boy" (page 92), "Wee Willie Winkie" (page 92), "A cat's tale, with additions" ("Three little kittens") (pages 93–95). The alphabet on Dover pages 93–95 has been omitted; "Jenny Wren" and "See, saw, sacradown" have been abridged. Several verses are placed on different pages from the Dover edition.

The presence of "Wee Willie Winkie," "Three Little Kittens" and "Hen, cock, cock, cock, cock" date the Hislop state securely from the middle 1840's at the earliest. "Wee Willie Winkie," written by a Scottish poet, William Miller, was first generally circulated in an English version in 1844. The other two poems were taken from Mrs. Follen's *New Nursery Songs*, dated circa 1843.

The Hislop state established several reprints by other publishers. Cottrell, around 1860, reprinted the inner text, but placed between pages [1] and 3 a seven-page reprint of an article from the *Boston Transcript* promulgating the Vergoose legend. This edition was either reproduced by stereotypy or some early photographic process from the Munroe and Francis standing type. It repeats all the earlier type defects, and shows the type-body in a further stage of degradation. Their title page reads THE ONLY TRUE/ MOTHER GOOSE/ MELODIES,/ WITHOUT ADDITION OR ABRIDGEMENT./ EMBRACING, ALSO, A RELIABLE / LIFE OF THE GOOSE FAMILY,/ NEVER BEFORE PUBLISHED./ NUMEROUS ILLUSTRATIONS. [old 1833 copyright notice] BOSTON: PUBLISHED BY C. W. COTTRELL,/ 36 Cornhill. In the copy in the New York Public Library, page 96 is blank. A handwritten note in the Boston Public Library copy of the Hislop state refers to another Cottrell edition in which the advertisement to *Chimes, Rhymes, and Jingles* appeared, calling it a "sequel." This is probably an earlier state.

Other publishers drew more or less heavily on the old Munroe and Francis *Mother Goose's Melodies*, and a list of other American Mother Goose books of the middle nineteenth century is largely a list of indebtedness to this book. Some publishers imitated the format and spirit, as the Appleton 1851 edition did; others assumed the old title and redrew illustrations from the original, like the Lippincott 1879 collection. Others simply reproduced the whole book. There are said to be such facsimiles by J. S. Locke of Boston and J. Miller of New York, neither of which has been accessible, but which seem to be reproductions of the Cottrell printings.

In 1905 Lothrop, Lee and Shepard published what purported to be "an exact reproduction of the text and illustrations of the original edition published and copyrighted in Boston in the year 1833 by Munroe and Francis." Edited by Mrs. Harriet Blackstone C. Butler with an introduction by Edward Everett Hale, this unfortunate venture printed the text and the extraneous introduction of Cottrell, but omitted pages 93–96. It is not a photographic facsimile; it is set in new type, with a new pagination.

DATES

While it is now certain that the first two printings of *Mother Goose's Melodies* occurred in 1833 and 1835, we have no definite dates for later printings. We can assume that the Hislop state appeared around 1845, what with datable inclusions and the style similarity of occasional new art work to *Chimes, Rhymes, and Jingles* (1845).

There is something very wrong about the Dover and Whitmore states of Family Two, however. They are internally inconsistent. Both states contain an advertisement for *Chimes, Rhymes, and Jingles*, which was copyrighted in 1845 and securely dates from 1845 or 1846. Yet the New York variants of the Dover state contain the imprint of C. S. Francis, which had no existence under that name after 1842. We have either a series of books published around 1845, with an incorrect publisher's name, or a series of books published several years earlier, advertising a book that did not exist.

The most obvious solution to this problem was proposed in 1938 by Codman Hislop, who was the first to recognize the dilemma of the advertisement, but was not aware of the C. S. Francis imprints or the diversity of Family Two editions. Mr. Hislop accepted the advertisement at face value and dated the later version[s] of *Mother Goose's Melodies* as 1845 or later, regardless of the copyright notice. To account for the incorrect wrappers, we might extrapolate from Hislop's position and suppose that the Boston printer in 1845 bound newly printed sheets into wrappers that had been printed previously and had been held in storage—at least three years, at most ten. This had to happen twice, since there are two such wrappers.

This is not an impossible situation. It is common to print "overages" of covers and use them later. But it is unlikely that two different sets of such New York wrappers should have been printed and stored. Other questions also arise. Under what circumstances were these wrappers printed and stored? For what edition were they intended if printed before 1842? We know of no printings between 1835 and 1845 except for the Brown state and the troublesome copies that are in immediate question. Were there other, lost or unrecognized printings of the book? Is there a hiatus between the Brown state and the Dover state printings, or was there a New York version of the Brown state which has not been found yet?

If the wrappers were stored (under any circumstances at all), why were they used without change? It would have been a small matter to run them through the press again, correcting the imprint. All in all, the solution of old wrappers and new pages presents many difficulties.

A second possible solution focuses on the advertisement for *Chimes, Rhymes, and Jingles* rather than on the wrappers. Is it possible that there was an earlier book of this title, later redesigned into the Billings and Hartwell 1845 volume? We have no evidence for this, and it is very unlikely. Or, can one assume, as a simpler solution, that the publisher kept announcing *Chimes, Rhymes, and Jingles*, hoping to have it ready, but did not really publish it until 1845? The announcement, which is not in the style of 1845, fits the contents of the published book, but it should also be noted that the four selections cited do not come from Halliwell (1843), and may have been in mind earlier than 1843. The announcement does not actually say that the book is ready.

Would a publisher announce a book before it is ready? It is done all the time, even today. It need not imply dishonesty, simply optimism, although a delay of from three to eight years strains one's faith.

Let us call this all a problem without present solution, although my suspicion is that the Dover state text is considerably earlier than 1845. New examples of the books in question—indeed, let us have the highest hopes and say dated copies of the books in question—may one day solve it.

Gratitude should be expressed to the Boston Public Library, Brown University Library, Library of Congress, New York Public Library, and Princeton University Libraries, as well as to the pioneer bibliographic work of William H. Whitmore, Codman Hislop, and Sinclair Hamilton.

E. F. B.